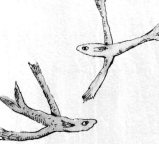

Visit us on the Web!
randomhousekids.com

Educators and librarians, for a variety of teaching tools, visit us at RHTeachersLibrarians.com

Library of Congress Cataloging-in-Publication Data
Magerl, Caroline, author, illustrator.
[Hasel and Rose]
Rose and the wish thing / written and illustrated by Caroline Magerl. — First American edition.
pages cm
"Originally published as Hasel and Rose in Australia by Penguin Books Australia Ltd., Melbourne,
in 2014" —Copyright page.
Summary: "Rose is a lonely face in a new town, but when she makes a wish to find a friend, the Wish Thing
starts a journey toward her from somewhere very far away." —Provided by publisher.
ISBN 978-0-553-53617-1 (trade) — ISBN 978-0-553-53618-8 (lib. bdg.) — ISBN 978-0-553-53619-5 (ebook)
[1. Wishes—Fiction. 2. Moving, Household—Fiction. 3. Friendship—Fiction.] I. Title.
PZ7.C7589Ro 2016 [E]—dc23 2015008078

MANUFACTURED IN CHINA
10 9 8 7 6 5 5 4 3 2 1
First American Edition

ose and the Wish Thing

A Journey of Friendship

Caroline Magerl

Doubleday Books for Young Readers

Rose was a new face in a new street.

And there was a new town right outside her window.

When the unpacking was done

and everything in its place,

Mama told stories with her hands and feet.

But when Rose was alone behind the door of her room, she looked out at things small and far away and she wished . . .

but the wish thing did not come.

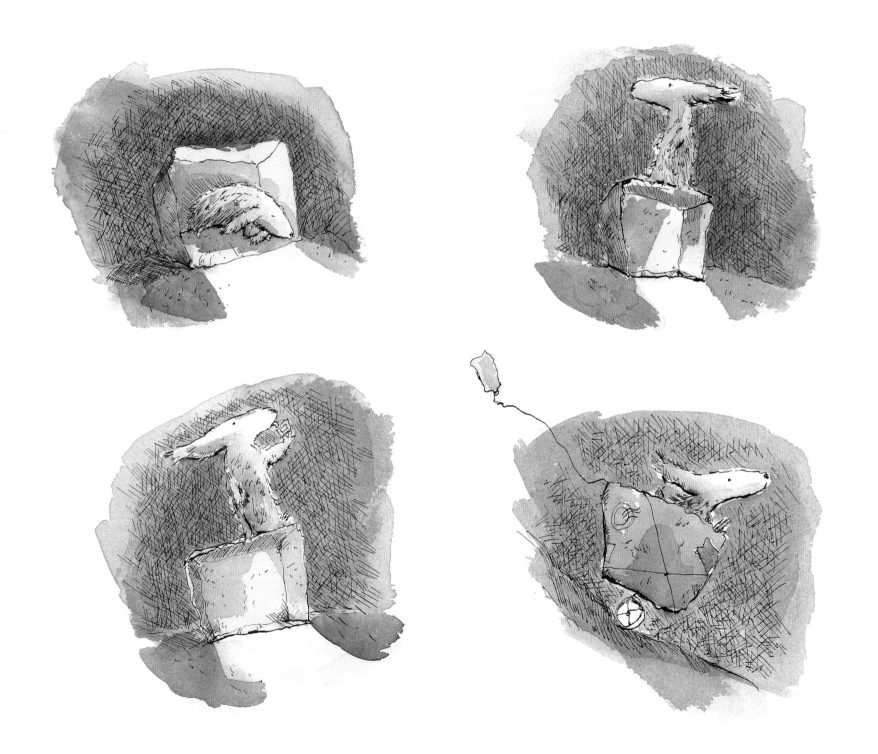

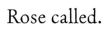

Rose called.

But the wish thing had no name.

Nothing could comfort Rose.

Not this . . .

And not this.

She drew a picture of the wish.

But she worried there was no such thing.

Everyone searched and searched.

Until at last they came to the sea.

They listened to the hush and growl of the waves.

The evening tide came with gentle fingers to roll over
the crabs and rock the stones.

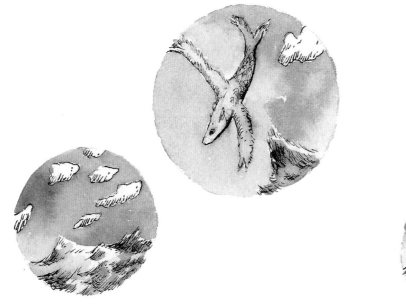

And there, nodding on the water, was a box.

It was a tired brown box.
The stamps hadn't been licked right to their corners.

Rose plucked it up out of the water.

She took the wish thing home . . . by cardigan.

It was made with tiny stitches,

and inside was a red glass heart for
finding things small and far away . . .

Or just outside the window.

And just down the stairs.

Out into a new street,

in a new town . . .

Where Rose and the wish thing
found some new old friends.